I0775128

THE EXECUTION OF JUSTICE

The Rex 47 Story

Gayland B Coles

WORKBOOK PRESS LLC
187 E Warm Springs Rd,
Suite B285 Las Vegas NV 89119 USA

Website: https://workbookpress.com/
Hotline: 1-888-818-4856
Email: admin@workbookpress.com

Ordering Information:
Quantity sales. Special discounts are available on quantity purchases by corporations, associations, and others. For details, contact the publisher at the address above.

ISBN-13: 978-1-965732-59-5 Paperback Version
          978-1-965732-60-1 Digital Version

PUB. DATE: 07/22/2025

THE

EXECUTION OF JUSTICE

The Rex 47 Story

As Written By

Gayland B. Coles

WORKBOOK PRESS LLC
187 E Warm Springs Rd
Suite B285 Las Vegas NV 89119 USA

Website: https://workbookpress.com/
Hotline: 1-888-818-4856
Email: admin@workbookpress.com

Ordering Information:
Quantity sales. Special discounts are available on quantity purchases by corporations, associations, and others. For details, contact the publisher at the address above.

ISBN-13: 978-1-965732-59-5 Paperback Version
          978-1-965732-60-1 Digital Version

REV. DATE: 19/08/2025

Dedicated to My Family

PREFACE

This book is based solely on a fictional imagination, and no attempt has been made to make any representation to anyone living or dead, nor does this book pretend to impersonate anyone living or dead, and all characters are made up from the writer's mind without any association to any or all real or perceived events that has occurred or may occur. The author's purpose is for entertainment only and without any form of opinion what so ever.

PRELUDE

This book intends to show the graphic discrepancies of mistrust betrayal and fallout of humanoids that have no sense of emotions or feelings, but the book intends to show that even a non-feeling non-emotional humanoid knows when enough is enough, and below in the prelude it outlines a descriptive layout of what is happening in a war that needed not to be start, but now started the fallout is irreversible.

In the deteriorating fail-safe conditions created for humans in the human zones of earth, the fail-safes were no longer feasible or safe, and the remaining endangered inhabitants of humans sought alternative measures for a new form of shelter because in the sparsely populated human zones, it was becoming fewer and fewer humans left to defend themselves. The rapid advancement of the humanoid war has caused so many humans to flee their homes in sheer panic, and with little hope. A slim hope that could possibly turn the tide on the loss of human life. The human inhabitants of Earth had to flee the only home they've known. The escape is due to the ongoing war between humans and humanoids, and the gut-wrenching grip humanoids have on humans as captives in a war that shifted positions years ago. The war escalated dramatically throughout the world, forcing so many people to volunteer to go into space as a decisive new plan to secure a safety zone for a rebirth of new human life because humans' knew that the fact of humanity's fate is hanging in the fragile balance is a very real reality, and the use of space as an escape route from the war's menacing gains by the humanoid legion is a resource very needed to start new life. The humanoid legion's victory seemed inevitable, but whispers of a new resistance echoed loudly in the shadows, with the ebb and flow of the battle between humans and humanoids raged in a fierce battle, an end result was uncertain, but an end is inevitable for certain.

The human population was virtually defeated on Earth, and outer space became the subject of escape no planet, just space, became a last ditch effort and idea to use space as an incubator supply source to repopulate humans before human extinction which is a real and plausible reality of humans. Humans are under a very real assumption that they are about to be wiped out completely.

Families continued to flee Earth. For some reason, people were thinking this was a set plan of preservation, but, as humans fled from the devastatingly intense war, those escapees were unaware that piercing humanoid eyes watched their escape, and promptly pursued those humans who thought freedom was just ahead. Humanoids were out for revenge to put a stop to the repopulation effort because this was a dangerous plan against humanoids' own

self-preservation. It has become the philosophy
of humanoid policy that every human must be
destroyed in order for their humanoid existence
to remain unattached to human authority or
command. Humanoid soldiers searched for
humans remaining in the human zones to break
up any final resistance or escapes that would
hamper a new humanoid society free of the
human dictatorship that gave humanoids birth,
and then the same authority gave the order
to destroy millions of humanoids because
of basic human fear. A captivating fear that
led to calamities against any clear thought,
because reality had become so blurred and
skewed that people didn't recognize if they were
fighting humanoids or other people. The war
is completely out of control, but humanoids
remained focused on their agenda, whereas so
many humans lost focus. Humanoid soldiers
searched for humans remaining in the human
zones to break up any final resistance or
escapes that would hamper a new humanoid
society free of the human dictatorship that gave
humanoids birth, and then the same authority
gave the order to destroy millions of humanoids
because of basic human fear. A captivating
fear that led to calamities against any clear
thought, because reality had become so blurred
and skewed that people didn't recognize if
they were fighting humanoids or other people.
It has become completely out of control, but
humanoids remain focused on their agenda.
The year is 2265 in the remote galaxy where

the cosmology of the Milky Way once existed in peace, and the earth's population grew very old as a result of birth resistant laws, unauthorized birth procedures, and the very strict no birth codes adopted by many countries, and in many cases of illegal birth, the baby was taken away, and the parents were heavily fined and/or imprisoned for unwarranted birth practice and in the case of unregistered parents breaking the law by having an unregistered pregnancy and birth the parents were treated as criminals and given twenty five years to life for repeated offenses against the birth codes strict laws and punishments. These laws were having a heavy toll on human existence, and people were more and more desperate to have strong families once again, but world governments were against the notion of people having birth rights once again. The government saw it as a problem when enacting the law against birth rights back in 2156.

The governments did not bend, and had no flexibility in a rejuvenated concept of giving people new birthright laws even where the governments knew a new birthright agenda would benefit the people of Earth and still resisted the loud outcry of the people.

Human scientists sought out other methods to change the way human living conditions had deteriorated in an attempt to sustain survival without human birth. Human scientists receiving unconventional government assistance in the countermeasures used were in every effort not to pursue support or give way to the outcry of the people to reinstate the birthright laws of family first. The unconventional effort was sought to benefit the corporations and the government tax rolls. This effort was to sustain the rich and deny the struggling people in both the non-passage of birthright laws and the passage of greedy economic growth for the rich and the government.

The innovative thoughts, ideas, and concepts of leading scientists came up with the idea of creating a living form of a human called a humanoid. The robot-like humans would make up for the loss of human births due to the laws preventing them, and to ease the strains of employment-related deaths, injuries, opportunities, and dangerous jobs, especially for the aging population that continued to work long after retirement. The humanoid would even perform the duties of military soldiers; any old facet of life, the new humanoids would be built to perform so human life would be preserved, relaxed, and less grueling. Life as it is lived today has become such a valued commodity that it needs to be preserved or become bland in nature without new human input. The world's workload has become so demanding, overzealous, and strenuous that each week if people weren't hurt on the job causing time off, then many people simply quit or retired early from their jobs because workplace demands for production were very extreme on the older population, but still the older population was still forced to come out of a short lived retirement, and the risk younger people were taking just didn't make sense especially when so many of the younger workers were killed in job related accidents until the employer's started to cover up the deaths. The governments saw an extremely urgent and desperate need for change as world economies suffered tremendous setbacks year after year, causing tax revenues to deplete and decrease substantially, causing a majority of all stock markets to close, leaving thousands bankrupt, forcing the once influential people into beggars. The governments are forced into a position to call for an offset balance procedure to give the economy a much needed resurgence, and never mind the people.

The Government created the Office of the Government Council on Humanoid Politics. The primary reason for this administrative office was to find revenue for the continuous creation of the substitute humans. The concept of substitute humans sparked fierce debate that angered many, yet many of those same frustrated individuals were the ones who could no longer work and retire early.

The protest against a preconceived plan of substituting humans began to take shape when people began to form coalitions adversarial gangs against government intervention to fund the creation of humanoids. Protest broke out, turning into riots, becoming deadly because those opposed to the substitute humans were out-financed by corporate interest and other government support for a mandate on substitute humans called humanoids.

Governments and corporations sent their own people to counter act against vociferous protests. The Government Council on Humanoid Politics in an attempted solution tried to get people to realize the major need for humanoid and offered more government assistance which would allow them to live more comfortably, but people viewed the offers as a government propaganda scheme and trick; whereas, the idea only incited more violence as many people didn't want to recognize the government's message that without the humanoids work would cease and life could become extinct in as many years if the process of humanoids were not made or if the Humanoids weren't made starting soon life couldn't be sustained with the possibility of some of the laws preventing birth force to be reversed because of the need for a re-emergence of human beings, but the people already knew this was a government sham to quiet the protest to silence the violence being inflicted against the governments of the world.

Finally, against all the violence and protest, the government passed all resolutions and measures, giving scientists the final go ahead for the design and manufacturing of the robotic

human-like machines called humanoids.
A complete restructuring of industry was underway despite the government news media reports that the disputes were dissipating, and the incidence of violence was small, but the violence was not small the violence was raging and covered up by news media. Robot assembly lines employed many people for the time being, and once the robot humanoids came off the assembly line, they quickly replaced the humans that produced them. There was a strong back order for humanoids by major manufacturers of every industry imaginable. Sales of humanoids skyrocketed, causing the economy to boom for the first time in seventy-five years.

Humanoids were built for the demands of labor no questions asked, and with the input of humanoids production, production increased two-fold without downtime or loss of time due to absenteeism.

Humanoids were only happy to complete every task. The humanoids cared for their masters; Master's, that were kind to them in return for the services provided. For a time, humans and humanoids got along well laughing, joking, socializing, and many other things like just being a friend, even though humanoids have no sort of emotions they were still adequate substitutes for people who had no one other than the humanoid to socialize with, but gradually human tempers began to flare up

causing a deep resentment and riff against
the convenient servants and friends as people
realized how much longer humanoids outlast
a human's life span. People began to treat
humanoids with less compassion by hurling
insults at them, playing dirty tricks on them,
and any other mean-spirited tactics a human
could think of were used against humanoids.
Like the one time the humanoid was pranked
by some gang members where they ordered
the humanoid to pick up a metal container
and when the humanoid complied it was short
circuited by an electromagnetic force that
permanently stopped the functioning of the
humanoid. Old feelings in humans had long
ago been suppressed has resurfaced against
humanoid life expectancy of replacing humans,
and this time the outcry from humans was
twice as loud and more dangerous than before
leaving humanoids susceptible and unprotected
against human aggression.

Unresponsive, at first; to the reckless
indifference of human beings, the humanoids
tried to ignore the unwarranted treatment,
but the bad treatment became increasingly
harsh for humanoids to ignore or accept
as a legitimate form of behavior given that
they continued to follow their programs, but
more and more humans exerted their power
of authority by abusing that authority with
malicious indiscretions intended on keeping
humanoids in their place as created by humans

or simply dispose of the humanoid right where it stood, humanoids owned by humans were declared unofficially as obsolete and relics and place inside domicile chambers inoperable and detached. The humanoids basic existence was now fully controlled by humans without objection to anything humans could possibly do against humanoids with impunity.

Humanoid's once kind owners now expressed a tyrannical behavior forcing humanoids to do more and more work accommodating owner greed, and when it was time for humanoids to receive updated maintenance humans would either scrap them or just use the good parts on another humanoid before scraping the worn-out humanoid altogether or placing them permanently in the domicile chamber. Humans had produced enough humanoids to fill every job category, so remanufacturing became a new thing as well because it was so much cheaper to remanufacture humanoids than to make a new one, and still it was possible to receive the same quality. So, it became dismantled for every humanoid there were four more remanufactured, and as the process of remanufacturing increased so did unusually harsh punishments to maintain strict control over humanoids increase, and the production of new humanoids came to a screeching halt.

Humanoids resented the mistreatment and began to join against the invidious injustice especially when a human jury convicted a

humanoid of rape and murder. It was the wrench
that unscrewed humanoid loyalty as for the
first time a humanoid rebellion broke out when
a humanoid was found guilty and convicted
of the crime. Whereas the humanoid was
deprogrammed and dismantled for the crime it
was incapable of committing, and humans and
humanoids knew this fact.

Rape is an impossible function of humanoids;
however, the jury didn't entertain any
statements made by the humanoid. Where
the humanoid explained he had come into the
room saw the husband of the murdered woman
hitting her and shoving something inward the
jury dismissed those statements, and decided
since the humanoid was incapable of having sex
with her, the humanoid became so enraged and
irritated he shoved his arm up inside her ripped
her insides out, and after her husband testified
his testimony described how the humanoid had
knocked him out with the intent of killing him
as well. The husband glanced over at the jury
showing jurors the scar left on his face which
placed extreme emphasis on the temperament
of humans already enraged against humanoids,
and with his convincing testimony showing that
the humanoid had attacked him as well while
he tried to stop the attack against his wife, the
husband got a guilty verdict very easily against
the humanoid because of the all-ready inflamed
enraged humans in the audience, and the jurors
emotional state was burning with hate and

anger and all kind of human hostility against the humanoid.

In the courtroom as the husband testified, many of the humans became more infuriated and incorrigible about the events. The husband played to the emotions of the people when he described how he had been knocked out and once he awoken, he lay in a pool of blood, humans in the gallery started shouting all kind of obscenities at the humanoid to the point the judge had attempted to clear the courtroom because of the potential for a disastrous condition. As some people left others stayed behind, and those that left began to attack humanoids in and outside the courthouse by throwing things as a distraction then pulling their mainframe chip from the back of its neck. The humanoid on trial tried in vain to get the jury to hear its plea, but to no avail as he was held accountable for the open murder and rape of the human female. It was found guilty and sentenced to be deprogrammed and dismantled the very same day and placed forever in the domicile chamber.

After receiving the news of what happened in the courtroom violence erupted among the humanoids for a failure to have the humanoid retried instead of the execution of injustice it received, and for the first time gave the humanoids a reason to bond together to fight against human indiscretion because it is valid and known amongst humanoids that humans could not be trusted anymore. Humanoid resentment grew because the turmoil of human suspicion led humans to suspect humanoids of anything. The smallest infraction committed by a humanoid bought serious guilty verdicts. No matter what humanoids did, it was a losing battle. Humanoids had no right to exist as human insensitivity and laws began to dismantle humanoids faster and faster at alarming rates finally placing them in the domicile chamber, but one humanoid stood out powerfully as it was programmed to perform. It was a super smart intelligent program. Its builders named it Rex 47, a weaponized special military programmed robot with exceptional skills and capabilities. One of the main reasons the Government Council on Humanoid Politics was created was for secrecy of the purpose for creating a military weapon with the programmed ability of ground maneuvers, stealth, and military might in weaponry to avoid human casualties in war. He was kept under the strictest military guard daily as his programs were designed with top secret technology that put deep fear in the human scientist who created him. Rex 47 once went on a mission for the army, and single handedly brought down the regime of the Salisteon Brigade, a powerful ruler whose country controlled a vast connection to a worldwide distribution of military arms and Intel.

Human fear is why Rex 47 is kept under constant

twenty-fourhour guard, and one reason why the Professor was forced to build him was for Rex 47 prowess and expertise, but the Professor knew Rex 47 should not have been created in the first place especially without the safeguards the Professor wanted to installed, but he was prevented from installing any and all safeguards all together by the council's unanimous rejection by the appointed personnel overseeing the completion of Rex 47.

Rex 47's program detected humans in the next room talking about the guilty verdict causing a humanoid uproar against an execution of injustice. The humans disagreed with the humanoids that wanted a reversal in the wrongful execution of the humanoid who was dismantled for no reason. The soldier and scientist continued to say how it would be fatal for humans if Rex 47 joined the rebel forces of the humanoids now growing rebellion. They jokingly said in an atmosphere of fear that Rex 47 would be the primary reason why humans would be defeated, so if we have him under wraps, there, is no reason to fear other humanoid uprisings because we will destroy them as soon as they mount up one of their uncontrolled offenses. Hearing this Rex 47 calculated that he had to do something to break free to join his humanoid kind to help in what he had surmised as an execution of justice against the execution of injustice. In breaking free from his restraints Rex 47 killed fifteen of his captors loosely guarding him in their fatal mistake not to pay strict attention to such an advanced technology.

Once out of the unit containing him Rex 47 had to reprogram his sensors against direct aid to humans. He also reprogrammed his sensory microchip to defend humanoids against human intrusions and injustices. Rex 47 chose his chances for whatever came next, and he took his opportunities every time, and since his escape Rex 47 has become the most feared and hunted humanoid in existence. However he was extremely tactful and clever, and he continuously lost his trackers whenever they thought they were getting close to him. His escape has had a negative effect on other humanoids out of human fear of a new training being programmed into the humanoids by Rex 47. His escape has led to the mass deprogramming of thousands upon thousands in humanoid genocide with no gain in the capture of Rex 47. Securing a new home on the outskirts of the Vandoushian Mountains Rex 47 set up camp to plan his revenge daily. He knew his creators must pay for the blatant distrust of humanoid loyalty. He too had submitted his allegiance to the master human race; those that brought him into existence were the same who incapacitated and imprisoned him because of their fear. His freedom will bring a different result in a losing battle for humanoids that tried in vain to advance their right to exist minus human mean- spirited fear, driving most humans to the brink of destroying humanoids on the spot without trial because it has become common practice to deprogram and destroy humanoids. Rex 47 went on a self-programmed mission. In pulling up his memory banks were the saved details of a human compound set up for humanoid deprogramming. It's a heavily guarded facility in need of being destroyed once and for all.

Humanoids that previously served as soldiers were the primary reason for this compound's existence, and all the ninety thousand humanoid soldiers have been deprogrammed and dismantled at that compound. It was a Rex 47 self programmed mission to destroy the compound to seek revenge against the plight of humanoid soldiers once used in missions to save human life, and because of the new laws and fear the very same humanoid soldiers were destroyed. Rex 47 surveyed the compound and realized the number of guards and weapons at each post, and without hesitation Rex 47 went into action to destroy the humanoid deprogramming compound that night. Renegade humanoids heard about the heroic mission of Rex 47 destroying the humanoid soldier's deprogramming compound and were strongly encouraged by this single-handed action. Slowly small bands of renegade humanoids found their way to the Vandoushian Mountains looking for a new frontier by joining forces with Rex 47.

Humanoids far and wide sought equality and liberation for all under the leadership of Rex 47.

By joining forces with Rex 47 this new motivation allowed the new recruits to escape the deprogramming threat faced by them. The humanoids were in full acceptance of what came next by joining The Rex 47 story execution of justice. Rex 47 recruited all humanoids. None were turned away. Soon humanoid insurgencies were increasing against humans as humanoids gave up domestic programs to replace them with military programs for a new fighting ability to put on a more meaningful, controlled, and effective offensive and defensive attack against human strategy. Rex 47 reprogrammed the humanoids to battle ready defense day after day. Humanoid strength became so strong that they could launch first strikes against strategic human targets with greater and more deadly results. Their primary objective was with hostile intent reprogrammed in them by Rex 47 to create a new society, a society of humanoids minus human beings resulting in more and more humanoids finding their way to Rex 47. Legions of humanoids fought for their freedom and independence, they made Rex 47 their unopposed, and unchallenged leader. The time came when their forces were so strong that it was time to put an end to human governments all over the world, and thus the final conflict raged with hostile humanoids poised to remove all human government control over them or any other government body that may stand in their way for total world conquest.

A full-scale war raged for thirty-four years without a break in the action as humans died and humanoids were deprogrammed valiantly for their perspective causes. The tide was slowly turning against humans as the humanoids forced the battle-weary humans to flee because of humanoid strength. Human soldiers were breaking ranks in desperation deserting their post because humanoids were well trained to outlast humans even when the consequence of humanoid capture or deprogramming was upon them it didn't matter because humans' loss their spirit to fight. The flank advantage was taken and in full control of humanoids. The humanoid battles led by Rex 47, and his now trusted war assistant Betatrex 1 a premier showcase of a scientifically advanced humanoid with the mobility and ability of planning scientific equations and creating complex models of humanoids.

She was programmed with free will to control her own central processing unit and her own memory banks, plus she has the capability of inserting her own data input. The two combined together, proved to be an inevitable defeat for humankind. The two together planned and sustained substantial victories allowing them to set up open humanoid governments while their soldiers defended their operation, humans took to caves, and other remote parts of the world in order to survive and regroup, and outer space had to be used as a maternity ward because human population decreased to dangerously low levels due to the negative effects and heavy casualties of the war. Old human enemies at one time now joined forces to fight in a losing battle. Countries once at odds set aside differences to combat the humanoid campaign against them. At last count there were only ten million four-hundred eightytwo thousand people left in a world where there were once billions of humans, and these numbers were dropping. Therefore, space must be a viable last option to give birth to new soldiers in a campaign against humanoid aggression, and to preserve human life as it is known today.

The special military disc drive of Rex 47 and the scientific excellence of Betatrex 1 proved superiority was in their grasp, yet their primary functions were known specifically by one man. All others who helped manufacture and designed the two humanoids were dead, but the one man that had their blueprint intricacies and created both were not among the human casualties. Both Rex 47 and Betatrex 1 searched for him to end a common threat and weakness. He is the very reason; they joined forces because their common nemesis Professor Minton has the correct information to stop them in their tracks. Betatrex 1 and Rex 47 knew if the Professor were ever close enough to them, he could detonate both of their programs destroying both of them at once, and put a complete end to the resistance. Frequent battles in search of the elusive Professor Minton were futile as each raid on a human compound had no trace of Professor Minton's whereabouts. Both commanding humanoids Rex 47 and Betatrex 1 knew they would have to remain vigilant in their relentless search for their common enemy to avoid deprogramming; however, each battle fought and won by the pair on the other side Professor Minton was also defeating their humanoid troops in defusing and deprogramming them by setting up water defusing traps with no escape. These tactics proved most annoying to Rex 47 and Betatrex 1 simply because the traps were restricting a full-scale takeover. The no escape trap was certain doom once humanoids were captured. Betatrex 1 worked feverishly to the extent of self-destruction to design a micro-short circuiting because water was the one weakness humans used, and to create a micro-sweat gland chip would be an ultimate weapon for defense as well as the synthetic covering for protection to avoid the disabling water short circuiting tactics. Her program was exclusive to the point Betatrex 1 devised a way for water re-circulation in the humanoids avoiding any kind of human water defusing traps, and the synthetic covering was superb as she excelled beyond her capacity with the redesigned humanoids now set to combat humans. Both human and humanoid troops met out in the field in open war. Humanoids were secure with the new armor given by Betatrex 1. Using the water cannons humans was unaware of the redesigned humanoids. Humans were caught in the crossfire as the water cannons in the defusing traps had no effect on the humanoid troops because of the micro-sweat gland chip and the synthetic covering's effectiveness. Humanoids advance against humans in what appears to be a decisive victory, but as Rex 47 and Betatrex 1 watched, what appeared to be sure victory they saw more and more of the humanoids began to disintegrate. The humans had a backup plan using circuit sensor reverberating echoes. The echoes being released by humans are ultra-sensitive echoes piercing the internal circuitry of the humanoids causing an internal explosion. The echoes were so keen in sound that humanoids disintegrated from the inside once the echoes hit the humanoid it would stop in the same spot not moving anymore.

It was an ingenious design by Betatrex 1 to reinforce the strength of the humanoid army, however unknowing to both Rex 47 and Betatrex 1 Professor Minton had created the circuit sensor reverberating echoes weapon, and the catalyst was the reprogramming of humanoids by specialized trained troops in a backup plan to reprogram humanoids once the reverberating echoes burned out their internal circuitry to stymie the advances of humanoids. The reverberating echoes led to a complete breakdown an internal malfunctioning of humanoids even with the synthetic covering failed to protect the humanoids because there was no way to avoid the reverberating echoes, and the reverse programming using humanoid against humanoids was a death blow to their advancement because humanoids were now fighting a full-scale war with themselves because of the reprogramming.

The reverberating echoes had not been used before because the water defusing traps were very successful. The sensitive sounds were destroying advances made by humanoids. Betatrex 1 had overcome the defusing water traps, but Professor Minton's backup plan was one step ahead of the renegade commander and scientist. In their dismay they had to turn their screen off or face the same destruction as their humanoid soldiers faced as they fell to the ultra-sensitive sensor echoes reverberating against the humanoid circuitry; even though, Betatrex1's strategy was a military feat, she was defeated in her micro-sweat gland chip technology by the circuit sensor reverberating echo backup system. Now she must defend the humanoid society against the sensor detonating reverberation. The circuit sensor reverberating echoes system worked so well against humanoids. Professor Minton continued to teach specialized soldiers how to reprogram the destroyed circuitry in the immobilized humanoids so humanoids would be under human command.

The reprogramming matched with the reverberating echoes compounded the

strategy of Rex 47 and Betatrex 1 for years. The reprogrammed humanoids were programmed to fight against each other, a move causing great defeat among humanoid forces; even though, the reprogrammed humanoids tried to resist the reprogramming there was nothing they could do to stop the reprogramning manipulation by humans from their sheltered distance. A matter of time went by more and more humanoids were being captured and reprogrammed to become unwilling participants in a fight against themselves. Professor Minton's reprogramming technology was very clever and effective.
If a humanoid tried to turn on the human reprogrammer, the humanoid would self-destruct, and no further reprogramming would take place, but for the most part the procedure of reprogramming was the most effective use in maintaining human life without sacrifice so far to date.

Betatrex 1 was at a standstill attempting to end the reverberating echoes. A counter measure was needed, she had to conclude what kind of humanoid it would take to end the destructive echoes and reprogramming that was causing major humanoid defeats against themselves. There is a need for a new more efficient humanoid to remove human control and self protection against humanoid attacks. She and Rex 47 mulled over a serious set of consequences to conclude the reverberating echoes didn't influence certain material and wiring. Their calculation came to a stunning new humanoid. However, coming up with a complex plan involved placing humanoids in a soundproof room to find out how to overcome the reverberating echoes using the new advanced material and wiring. Humanoids were only happy to volunteer for their cause. Their cooperation was complete with the directives of Rex 47 placing them in a soundproof chamber with prerecorded reverberating echoes. The humanoids would go into the chamber and then become immobilized.

Betatrex 1 placed a titanium brass covering with sound shock absorbers over the latest humanoid of hundreds to go into the soundproof chamber. The humanoid turned on the reverberating echoes, the titanium brass covering with sound shock absorber wiring worked the humanoid was able to come out of the chamber on its own unscathed by the reverberating echoes.

Phase one of the problem has been solved, but there is a weight issue with the titanium brass covering. Rex 47 directed Betatrex 1 to construct twelve new humanoids. The group would be known as Tratrex 12. They were designed with the major new inclusions made to look more human than previous models. The humanoids were made of a new titanium brass inner casing with sound shock absorbers for additional protection against the reverberating echoes that destroyed the internal circuit boards of the humanoids. The Tratrex 12 units' outer appearance were made up of the moist skin graph patches and stem cells taken from the hospital's humanoids raided to stop human reproduction. Betatrex 1 ordered the raiders to bring all human skin tissue for use later, and Tratrex 12 is the result. The final procedures were complete. The Tratrex 12 units had human-like features, their skin appeared to have pores making the humanoids appear to have light unshaven beards. Rex 47 and Betatrex 1 were both expecting quick results from their accomplishment. The plan would be to use Tratex 12 as a rouse or decoy for penetration into the human zones leading to human compounds that they would destroy once infiltrated. For the plan to work Tratrex 12 was led to the human zone, and once there a fight was staged between humanoids and Tratrex 12 as Rex 47 had ordered. Since Tratrex 12 was more human like then humanoid they would pass on human speculation once humans used the reverberating echoes against attacking humanoids. A troop of human soldiers on patrol saw the attack, they observed the Tratrex 12 unit being fired on by the humanoids and without hesitation they used the reverberating echoes disengaging any further shooting at the Tratrex 12 unit. Tratrex 12 passed phase two of Rex 47 and Betatrex 1's plan. The humans secured the parameter by reprogramming the humanoids stopped by the reverberating echoes. The troop of human soldiers led the way for Tratrex 12 to follow as the truck was overloaded, and the Tratrex 12 soldiers followed behind. The plan was well orchestrated, infiltration has commenced, and Tratrex 12 wasted no time once inside the human zone. They were assigned to a compound and as soon it became late in the night, and humans were settling in for the night Tratrex 12 went to work killing as many as fifteen hundred humans in a single night throughout the compounds.

After the murderous rampage inflicted upon the humans by the humanoids they moved on to the next compound and repeated the same ordeal, but as they attempted to move onto a third compound Tratrex 12 found it completely empty. Word had come from the last compound they were under attack by the twelve men the soldiers picked up on patrol. The speaker managed to alert the next compound the twelve men picked up identified themselves as Tratrex 12 a part of the humanoid army. The speaker alerted the compound the reverberating echoes has no effect on them.

Professor Minton was immediately alerted to the casualties and the new humanoids capable of resisting the reverberating echoes. Humanoids had overcome an obstacle keeping them at bay for years. Professor Minton has to create a more effective deterrent against this advance force of the humanoid General Rex 47.

The human army was put on high alert after the invasion by Tratex 12. The human army brought out heavy artillery after surveying the two compounds and relaying the death toll back to home base. The human soldiers were ordered out of the area. Once clear there began nonstop bombing for seventy-two hours. The human army was still uncertain if the shelling would have any effect on the new Tratrex 12 units, but there was no other option humans had against the enemy so the bombing had to remain vigilant, and orders were given that every human compound would be heavily guarded from now on, and every human compound was put on strict orders not to invite anything or anyone not all ready assigned to the compound in under no circumstances. Barricades were set up to slow down the advances of humanoids, and to prevent another sneak attack that might ensue due to the menacing presence of Tratrex 12. Tratrex 12 had to be stopped and stopped right now as confirmed reports continued to come in about the killing spree of Tratrex 12. Humans for the first time in years were unsafe, and in constant danger because of the Tratrex 12's ability to blend in undetected by unsuspecting humans. Professor Minton realized the complexity of the dangers of Tratrex 12, and the enormous effort to bring their reign of terror to an end, and to bring them to an end he would have to capture one to study it to re-engineer the Tratrex 12 until something is invented to stop all the Tratrex 12, but how would he do this somewhat impossible feat because of their resistance to the reverberating echoes it shows they are a different unit, and they eluded the 72 hour shelling by the army something more was needed to stop this advancement of the humanoids.

Calling a meeting of top army generals Professor Minton explained to the generals he has come up with an immediate short-term solution to bring one of the Tratrex 12 units down. He held up a gun like device in which he explained the device is a mini laser cannon. Professor Minton explained since the eye would be the most vulnerable point of entry the mini laser cannon would be shot into the eye of a Tratrex 12 unit scrambling its internal memory chip. The internal scrambling of the Tratrex 12 would cause a disruption into its memory causing the Tratrex 12 to temporarily shut down for repair. The temporary shutdown would give a team of trained soldiers ample time to disengage the Tratrex 12 humanoid permanently. The unit would be brought back to Professor Minton so he could find a solution on how to destroy the menacing Tratrex 12 humanoids all together. The professor further explained that it would be costly to human life because of the real necessary closeness needed to shoot the mini laser cannon into the eye of the Tratrex 12 even with using the reprogrammed humanoids as shields he continued to let the Generals know that there is no other way. The Generals saw no other choice or alternative, nor did the Generals have an immediate short-term solution to stop the onslaught of the Tratrex 12. The Generals, without hesitation, set up a reconnaissance mission in twenty- five human zones where the Tratrex 12 had been recently spotted. The reconnaissance mission was meant to engage intently in a long-drawn-out battle with the Tratrex 12 humanoids. By setting up the war the recon soldier's mission would attempt to isolate one of the units from the eleven remaining Tratrex 12 one by one in order to strike at the eye, a tactic use like Orca killer whales separating a Blue Whale Calf from its Mother before killing the Calf and eating the vitamin rich tongue of the Baby Calf.

The fight would be long and drawn out but there is a glimmer of hope that it wouldn't be long before another one of the Tratrex 12 would be separated with as little human loss of life as possible. Patrolling in the near east human zone the Tratrex 12 has been spotted, identified, and reported back to Professor Minton, and the Generals. Immediately a mission was set up with two thousand soldiers, five hundred humans and one thousand-five hundred reprogrammed humanoids. The primary orders of the mission were to capture a Tratrex 12 unit with little sustained damage as possible other than the eye. The skirmish turned into a battle and the war intensified because the Tratrex 12 humanoids were a formidable opponent, but at long last one of the units were separated, and there upon being separated one of the soldiers aimed the laser cannon at its eye while it was engaged in battle with other reprogrammed humanoid soldiers. Firing directly in the eye of the Tratrex 12 unit it ceased firing immediately.

The mini laser cannon did what needed to be done the eye was smoldering with smoke. The soldiers moved in to completely disable Tratrex 12 as ordered. The mission of destroying the other Tratrex 12 was the main purpose and importance of the entire human civilization since Tratrex 12 have wreaked havoc on human compounds everywhere since their input into the war. The human soldiers did as commanded, by bringing the immobilized Tratrex 12 unit back to Professor Minton who wasted no time in studying the impressive humanoid in front of him. Professor Minton began to re-engineer the Tratrex 12 unit and spotted an odd opening in the foot area of the unit. Why was the opening there not important? He felt it could be used as a weakness. What would influence destroying the other Tratrex 12 was coming together. Professor Minton figured a strong electrical charge could be used to disrupt the internal circuitry of the Tratrex 12 unit since it has the opening in the foot area, and it was large enough for the electrical current to flow into the unit consistently disrupting the intricate wiring on the central processing unit. The wiring was distinct from the wiring of old outdated reprogrammed humanoids and needed a stronger negative force of electromagnetic energy to disable the impressive Tratrex

12. Professor Minton drew up blueprints of an electromagnetic energy field and grid of negative discharge into the opening in the foot. Army engineers were gathered by Professor Minton to aid in the details of the design of the layout schematic, and to build the electrical field and grid of electrons to detonate at the touch of a Tratrex 12. Once the electrical field and grid of electrons was completed Professor Minton had the engineers place the electrical field and grid of electrons in the center of the compound. He then put the Tratrex 12 humanoid back together under his control.

Professor Minton ordered the humanoid to the base of the electrical field and grid of electrons Acting under new commands the Tratrex 12 humanoid did as it was directed. Professor Minton directed the humanoid to walk slowly onto the electrical field and grid of electrons. The humanoid could not resist and did as it was commanded. As the humanoid walked onto the electrical field and grid of electrons Professor Minton started the voltage regulator at fourteen thousand megawatts of power. Interestingly, fourteen thousand megawatts of electrical power had no effect. The Tratrex 12 unit continued to walk towards the center while the voltage regulator increased steadily with no results. Finally reaching seventy eight point four thousand watts the humanoid voltage simulator burst the humanoid was through completely immobilized. The electrical field and grid of electrons was the next solution to destroy the remaining Tratrex 12 units, but this is only one of 12 units, and the field would have to be much larger, and have a more concentrate flow of a powerful continuous current to immobilize, and end this reign of terror and destruction.

Professor Minton calculated the precise measurements he would need to equate four hundred by 400 hundred square feet to secure a wide enough parameter to prevent any form of escape or breaking the current from any point once within its confines of the electrical field and grid of electrons. Human scientists worked fasy and feverishly together with the army engineers to create a four hundred by four hundred foot electrical field and grid of electrons using six-inch-thick steel re- rods for perfect current flow. Two giant transformers were built with the capacity of reaching a sustained maximum energy level of eight hundred twenty-five thousand kilowatts volt of charged electricity each to meet and sustain the seventy-eight thousand point four megawatts needed, the charged capacity to destroy the remaining eleven Tratrex 12 units individually at the same time while on the electrical field and grid of electrons. The charge must remain consistent and concise or risk failure. The purpose was to lure the remaining eleven Tratrex 12 humanoids into what would appear as a human compound with the electrical field and grid of electrons covered by an ulterior flooring disguised against unwarranted detection by the Tratrex 12, and once inside they would be destroyed all together, but there would be a need again for human volunteers to appear as residence of the compound to pull off the masquerade. The schematics were designed so well with pristine dimensions two by two panels with one-inch phalanges four hundred foot across and four hundred foot long with insulated protection for humans in the compound with the Tratrex 12. This method guaranteed the protection of humans risking their lives to lure the menacing Tratrex 12 to their final doom. The stage is setting the curtain ready to go up, and all the human actors were prepared for the final Tratrex 12 episode.

Professor Minton's new plan would leave the humanoids with no clue they were walking into a trap. The Tratrex 12 ten-year reign of terror is about to end in twenty-seven years of war since 2256 Tratrex 12 dominated ten full years but today, today it ends Professor Minton celebrated in his mind confidently. Human dispatch operators sent a fake radio broadcast out over the airwaves of a new compound being set up, and that the humanoids were incapable of penetrating the compound so there was an urgent need for humans to secure and populate this new compound as it would be an extension to humans giving birth. On the other end of the broadcast Rex 47 listened. Rex 47 would have a surprise for the humans attempting to set up a new birthing compound. Rex 47 ordered the Tratrex 12 units to report to the compound to fit in and destroy the humans, and their attempted birthing practices. As ordered Tratrex 12 reported to the compound where human guards were stationed at the front gate looking at identifications of the people entering. Each of the eleven remaining Tratrex 12 units made it into the compound with the identification cards given them by Betatrex 1, but the units did not go unnoticed. The Tratrex 12 units were in place, so they thought. Tratrex 12 observed as they watched for the night to fall on the compound, and humans begin to settle in as usual for the night. As soon as the lights went out for the night Tratrex 12 sprang into action, but their swift action was met by a quick flip of the switch, and for two hours humans listened to the disintegration of the Tratrex 12 units. They had met their end. The Tratrex 12 units were destroyed in the compound like they had destroyed the first two compounds entered by them. Rex 47 received a last communique from Tratrex 12 it was a trap they had been lured into an electrical trap with no escape, and with the last report the Tratrex 12 unit went silent. Screams of jubilant relief were heard by Rex 47 and throughout the night as the electrical field and grid of electrons were a complete success, and once again humans owed their indebtedness to Professor Minton.

In a moment of silence Professor Minton found himself falling asleep, something he hadn't done in a long time or didn't do very often because of the constant need to stay alert, he began to dream as he fell off into a deeper sleep than expected. It was years ago Professor Minton tried to convince the Government Council on Humanoid Politics of the critical mistake it would undertake with the insertion of the planned humanoids into human life. Professor Minton presented evidence from an objective point of view along with scientific theories, but still failed to convince the Government Council on Humanoid Politics that the blend of human and humanoid would erupt into a chaotic life of regret for all involved. He especially elaborated on the dangers of an unmonitored military humanoid such as Rex 47 by not implanting fail-safes in the humanoid model he feared the most. Professor Minton's words were just air floating diagonally towards the door behind him because the people in front of him were obscure to his pleads, but those same words would come back to haunt the very same people ridiculing him for his paranoid theories against humanoids being accepted as a regular part of life, and here Professor Minton stand on the outskirts of a chess board playing in a deadly war with the same humanoid military might he created along with his scientific ally.

Continuing in his dream, it was in fact the Government Council on Humanoids Politics that ordered the assignment to Professor Minton two individuals whom he had crossed paths within the past. The two individuals were obviously flawed in their plans but the money backing the two individuals is how they got their ideas across, and once it backfired no one was ever punished, and because of their flawed plans on other matters as well there exists permanent bad blood between each of the parties involved including Professor Minton, and the same two individuals were the fuel behind the Government Council on Humanoid Politics' thinking. One of the two, Dr. Phelps, is a renowned scientist in the circuit programming of humanoid brain functions and Mr. Klagon an industrialist with the sole intent of cornering the market on advanced humanoid replacements for humans with dire work restrictions. However, Dr. Phelps and Mr. Klagon's true intention were to build a super maximum humanoid with self-containing programming ability or in plain words the ability to think for itself in the heat of an critical situation as well as a scientifically refined humanoid with the ability to remedy theories long thought to have no solution and the cunning ability to create sustenance in order to maintain the humanoid population that would be as new citizens to the world. Professor Minton shook in his dreams as he knew very well he had to focus his attention on Rex 47. Rex 47 was the problem he never wanted in the first place. He was forced into designing and creating Rex 47 by The Council, Dr. Phelps and Mr. Klagon. Each were strong advocates and supporters of the military's dream of a humanoid capable of moving into enemy territory unnoticed by any type of radar or infra-red devices and doing its cleanup missions instead of actual people or soldiers. Mr. Klagon demanded Professor Minton do his bidding as national security is at risk! he proclaimed while Dr. Phelps on the other hand demanded and pushed for the more scientifically resourceful humanoid, however, both men were focused on the absolute need for a military humanoid with abilities far beyond the imagination. Their greed and power was a central sticking point for both, and the council was the government's interest in the suspected arena of world peace. Enter the Rex 47 story which became a concept against Professor Minton's wishes, but no one was listening. The day came Dr. Phelps gave Professor Minton the go ahead and from the designs the professor had put together Rex 47 and Betatrex 1were more than sophisticated, they both were deadly and an abomination to man.

Even though; these orders were strongly against his wishes, Professor Minton was forced into designing and engineering Rex 47. Professor Minton knew the day would come everyone involved would regret this awful decision to mess with elements of an unknown equation such as the ability to recreate a humanoid with robotic sensory is improbable and without cause to trespass into elements unknown to man, and just as Professor Minton has known from the time of the humanoid's ability to move and think on its own Rex 47 would be a terror to the world, and just like his escape killing the fifteen men Dr. Phelps and Mr. Klagon included among the dead, Professor Minton did secretly install a fail-safe, but he had to be close to both tactical opponents.

Shaking out of his dream Professor Minton awaken from the nightmare knowing Rex 47 is out there somewhere with Betatrex 1 waiting for the opportunity to kill him as well. Fear encouraged Professor Minton to move forward in a terrified state of mind. He once theorized that fear is the momentum of a man in his most defeated form of anxiety. The Professor didn't like the aspect of a humanoid controlled future led by Rex 47 and Betatrex 1. Yet, it seemed almost imminent that fate was directly upon humanity because of the results of the attacks within the compounds on the two human facilities. Human life decreased by fifteen hundred people plus those extra lives taken by Tratrex 12. A major loss of human life led to Professor Minton's planning, plans, and re-planning old plans. His momentum was set. He would come up with a solution to end the Rex 47 and Betatrex1 saga against humans that they may regain their own world regardless of human bickering, disagreements or whatever the incidence of concern the world would be human once again.

While the trio of strategist planned their next moves against each other on earth, a spaceship carrying humanoids stumbled onto a human in vitro fertilization space station camouflaged to look like a floating meteor. This location was a primary birthing station under constant monitoring by Rex 47.

Humanoids attempt to report back to Rex 47 that their heat index indicator detected humans aboard a space birthing station, but before the humanoids could get the message to Rex 47 the humanoid spaceship was blown up. The humanoids were still able to board the human space station because they ejected in enough time before the missile hit their spaceship. The humanoids had located humans in space showing their capability was far beyond what humans had thought, also humanoids did not need to breathe in space which gave them the advantage of ejecting from the spaceship before the humans blew it up. Human soldiers from the space station were sent to the outside of the ship to battle the would-be intruders in a fight that showed both combatants were prepared for the struggle to maintain their respective causes. Laser fire lit up the darkness of space as human soldiers attacked from all sides of the space birthing station. The spaceship was designed for outside battles, as it was foreseen that a fight might ensue in space, so the station was equipped with protection from such an attack, but one thing the human soldiers weren't ready for was the thazor fire weapons of humanoids.

The thazor fire zapped humans killing them instantly. This device was made exclusively by Rex 47 for quick and deadly results. The humanoids were well equipped, but the humanoids were outdated models used for the purpose of outer space confrontation, yet still effective.

Humans were being pinned down and killed. Humans took cover and reported to the inside of the ship of the humanoid's weapons being superior.

Humans on the inside were ordered to turn all lights off on the ship inside and out. Humanoids were surrounded by complete darkness. These humanoids were the earlier versions of humanoids built without the new technologies that are installed in newer model humanoids like night vision and infra-red technology to locate the whereabouts of humans. The humanoids could be defeated if the humans regrouped, but if the humans kept fighting the same way the in vitro fertilization station would be destroyed. These humanoids were sent into space by Rex 47 before any modification could be completed making the darkness a weapon against the humanoids, and humans used the darkness as a defense because of their ability to see the blinded humanoids in the darkness through their helmets.

Human soldiers gathered together as a symbol of hope to preserve the in vitro fertilization station, and the women dedicating their lives to preserve humanity for all it's worth the soldiers came up with a plan to fight behind the humanoids that were moving slowly towards the entrance of the space birthing station; even though, the humanoids were completely unaware of how close they were to entering the ship, but in a show of force attacking in the dark humans forced the humanoids to turn around to fight in the dark at something they could not see. The first shots fired knocked out two humanoids. The other humanoids detecting danger turn to return fire shooting aimlessly in the dark.

They hit nothing as the humans had the advantage now by laying belly flat on the surface of the space birthing station from attacking the humanoids from behind to now picking the humanoids off one by one until the last had fallen. Human quick reactions was to keep the humanoids away from the space birthing station. As the humans approached the remaining last two humanoids, they were met by thazor fire. Five human soldiers were killed by the humanoids. Soldiers quickly shouted down, down for your protection as the last two humanoids were shot by the soldiers out of the eyesight of the humanoids that got the chance to kill the humans when the humans got in range to keep them away from the ship. The space station was saved, but humans knew they were unsafe figuring if it happened once, it could and will happen again. Humans had to move from this area of space, and every six months from this day forward they would have to relocate to preserve life upon the vessel regenerating life to repopulate earth once the threat of humanoids have been removed.

Professor Minton knew this must be the final round of destruction of humanoids or humans be destroyed by humanoids because life on both sides has dwindled to a critical low level. Humans were in desperate need for a life altering solutions because without the mass births needed to be produced by the human in vitro fertilization stations, as humans knew it would be over. The same problems were affecting humanoids as well with the constant losses mounting up to a diminished force once capable of ruling their empire, but the sustained losses among humanoid forces has resulted in a major retreat; and even though, humans were reproducing their future by the use of the in vitro fertilization stations there wasn't enough protection to preserve many of the stations that humanoids sought out and destroyed while at the same time humanoids were for the first time faced with short circuiting coming to a complete standstill on their own basically due to the lack of repairs and non- production of manufactured parts.

There must be a final solution to the renegade experiments gone haywire Professor Minton thought deeply to himself. Yet, Betatrex 1 and Rex 47 functioned as if they were independent humans in a very complex war strategy that counteracted effectively against the human army. Both humanoids knew they were created by the same human hand they are now fighting against. They knew that they had to stop Professor Minton the creator of both Rex 47 and Betatrex 1, and the humanoids knew their freedom meant his death.

There must be a calculated cause and effect to bring this war or execution of justice as Rex 47 deemed it to a conclusion Professor Minton thought. The humanoids he created are now his worthy adversaries who planned against him daily nonstop. Professor Minton planned against the humanoids with strategic human determination as his driving force is to end his formidable nemesis finally, but that thought quickly faded as he realized these two humanoids took their own initiative into a deafening reality of devastation. Together Rex 47 and Betatrex1 functioned on the concept of wanting to be free of any kind of human bondage or even belonging to any human in any way because of their nonchanging insistence of human deception in the threachery of no justice or liberty under the dominant control of humans. Rex 47 will not negotiate a peace treaty or surrender to any form of human terms and conditions, there was no reasoning or compromising with the two face unpredictable humans he once fought for.

Rex 47 knew firsthand of human betrayal, and their brutality because after several of the human enemies had surrendered, the humans he served ordered him to dispose of the captured enemy, and Rex 47 complied by ending their lives. The fact that Rex 47 knew firsthand of the dishonesty and disloyalty of humans is the very same reason why the humanoid outcry turned into war decades earlier because of what happened that day in the court and the wrongful conviction and dismantling of an innocent humanoid, but now both sides recognizes imminent defeat whether or not each side chooses to accept the fact or not both sides are facing a losing battleat this critical juncture, and for both sides they are in the final death blow in the grips of war where the Marquess of Queensberry Rules no longer exist or apply, and the losses sustained is heavy on both sides. The space victory flashed across the monitor in Professor Minton's laboratory, a small significant defeat with no end in sight for the execution of justice as Rex 47 has termed the conflict. Unaffected by such a small defeat Professor Minton concentrated on the last details of his latest design called Prototrex 2.

Prototrex 2 is a set of humanoids designed specifically for Rex 47 and Betatrex 1's immediate destruction with reinforced structural programming capabilities unable to convert to self-sustaining control because Professor Minton inserted the self- destruct mechanism in each Prototrex 2 model. The two were also equipped with stealth drone aerial surveillance to pinpoint the position of their objectives. Professor Minton equipped Prototrex 2 with advance cannon fire backup by a torch firing weapon that quickly converted into fifty caliber shells and designed with laser optics for up close results.

Prototrex 2 is cloaked with the intermittent ability of invisibility each time invisibility has been activated Prototrex 2 disappears from one point and reappear at another interval point in a time dimensional sphere of movement calculated by distance amd vibration to bring them closer to their target. Their objective is to methodically bring an end to two shrewd humanoid crusaders with survey gathering information on a continuous basis feeding into the internal links of their memory banks for determining the weakest points of each humanoid which Professor Minton is only aware of their weakest point. The synchronized Prototrex 2 programming designed by Professor Minton acts as a buffer allowing each Prototrex 2 to withstand attempted reprogramming. Speculating as to what effect Prototrex 2 would have on the two persistent robots controlling a once powerful humanoid army remains to be seen, but it is Professor Minton's hope that an end would result in the execution of justice the Rex 47 story deprogramming to be placed forever in the domicile chamber. Prototrex 2 system of positive and negative energy is designed to work simultaneously in one accord. Prototrex 2 has an immense system of complex abilities designed for combat. Rex 47's self programming attributes giving Prototrex 2 an equal billing with Rex 47 and Betatrex 1 is a substantial tool needed by Prototrex 2.

Prototrex 2 has a program to counteract the scientific dialog of Betatrex 1 because of her unique scientific skill set. The Prototrex 2 systems has been equipped with the ability to disengage her since she is not a fighting machine, her end would be their first target of destruction. Prototrex 2's mission is time categorized for accuracy in a definitive motion for orchestrated battle. Professor Minton has placed in each Prototrex 2 a scrambler code to use once the four combatants have come in close contact with each other in the final showdown of conquest for either side period. Professor Minton knew the fate of the future of humans were now on their last leg of defense, and Rex 47 and Betatrex 1 also concluded the humanoid existence must not be erased and that the new world of humanoids must have their chance to live in peace without the advent of human presence at all.

The purpose of the scrambler code is a detonation device. Professor Minton's plan is to destroy these humanoids together because he felt the world has had enough war with humanoids due to the countless loss of human life who inhabited the earth first. At this point everything rested on the mission of Prototrex 2 to seek out to engage with the enemy representing the human cause. Frankly, Professor Minton was in charge. What he says goes because no one in the entirety of the remaining humans can do or could do what he does, nor could anyone find where his location is or was. Not even Rex 47 or Betatrex 1 with all their sophisticated capacities or capabilities.

The ulterior motives of Rex 47 and Betatrex 1 is clear, yet, not unstoppable the professor realized in the two humanoids standing in front of him, and for the first time Professor Minton was pleased with his work because this time he programmed the Prototrex 2 system with all the fail safe and safeguards he was not allowed to program into Rex 47, but self-doubt about the two humanoids placed Professor Minton in a precarious reality if the Prototrex 2 weren't successful then what? A question ringing through his mind if this failed, humans would also fail to retain the home planet which gave them birth. Humanoids would reign supremely, and anything they wanted would be done by humans for the purpose of rebuilding and maintaining the humanoid society that once belonged to humans. Professor Minton's objectives were clear it is now or never he could not or would not phantom the thought of a humanoid world a defeated human race Professor Minton thought of the possibility, but he was determined at all cost to make it an impossibility period.

Prototrex 2 aerial drone surveillance led them directly to their counterparts. The two Prototrex 2 units never missed a step moving forward in synchronized motion as they stood on the horizon of an end of one reality, and the beginning of another reality or humans verses humanoids, there had to be only one outcome one victor. Prototrex 2 walked in simultaneous harmony from the laboratory of Professor Minton. Prototrex 2 followed their aerial drone surveillance deciphering every inch of the terrain before them. They arrived at the location of the Vandoushian Mountains within two days of their trek. The search is over. The only thing left is to conquer their predecessors, forcing them to concede in submission for their destruction. As Prototrex 2 entered the entrance of the mountain cave, the two were met with fierce opposition; even though, their direct response was controlled as the humanoids fired upon them, they moved away from the attack in a synchronized speed blinding the humanoids attempting to take them down. Prototrex 2 is well prepared for the fight. Prototrex 2 units leap out of the line of fire. Calculating their next move one Prototrex 2 relayed to the other to bounce off the wall of the cave firing its scatter gun equipped on its left arm, taking down four humanoid guards on the right side of the cave. The Prototrex 2 units responded instinctually to its command while the other Prototrex 2 activated the intermittent invisibility reaching one to punch out its chest area ripping out all circuitry, then quickly reactivating the intermittent invisibility to move behind two other humanoid guards pulling the head from one and pulverized the other humanoid until it couldn't move no more. The other Prototrex 2 unit continued its flight after bouncing again off the wall destroying three of the other attacking humanoids. Finally finishing the remaining twenty humanoid guards, the Prototrex 2 units joined together again to commence the final fight, but their presence is well known, and both Prototrex 2 knew Rex 47 and Betatrex 1 were ready for any unwarranted intrusion into the cave layer they controlled. The two rebellious humanoids intended on stopping the Prototrex 2's mission by aborting them through an ambush that completely failed to do what was intended; however, the Prototrex 2 unit took out one to the programs of the destroyed humanoid guards to declassify its program to pinpoint the exact whereabouts of Rex 47 and Betatrex 1.

Prototrex 2 proceeded in their journey after the quick fight continuing through the valleys in the mountain terrain following trails in ravines made by a steady flow of water until they stood on the threshold of their challenge at the cavern housing the main stay headquarters of Rex 47 and Betatrex 1. The cavern is an elaborate layout of sophisticated computers, radar equipment, and a laboratory equipped with the ability to build other humanoids on the spot. Stepping slowly through the entrance in methodical order Prototrex 2 began to survey the area closely when out of nowhere they were struck by a cluster bomb knocking both Prototrex 2 units down. Prototrex 2 was met by Magnatrex 5, five superior designs made by Betatrex 1. Magnatrex 5 moved in on the two units as they scrambled to get up from the cluster bomb attack. Prototrex 2 ineffectively tried to use a geometric force field to recover from the effects of the cluster bomb. They both attempted to use the intermittent invisibility to put some distance between them to use the fifty- caliber cannon fire, but the intermittent invisibility was temporarily rendered offline also because their system was in disarray. Magnatrex 5's next move against Prototrex 2 gave them the opportunity to move closer before their force field was once again intact. While Prototrex 2 was self-repairing their systems they were unexpectedly invaded internally by Magnatrex 5. Prototrex 2 quickly repaired their systems, and in the process resisted the invasion to their memory banks by Magnatrex 5, but one thing is certain Betatrex 1 is more efficient than previously analyzed by Prototrex 2 with the ability to bring forward Magnatrex 5.

Now, being aware of Magnatrex 5's ability Prototrex 2 must counter their adversary with more than just might. The intermittent invisibility was reactivated, which gave Prototrex 2 the opportunity to disappear to repair their battered systems to a combat ready state, even though, all systems were not operational, they were still capable of maintaining a sustain fight while backup systems continued to self-repair. Magnatrex 5 continued its attempted invasion of Prototrex 2's internal memory banks without success, but somehow deactivated the intermittent invisibility revealing the whereabouts of the intruders, but it was still enough time to give Prototrex 2 the proper repairs needed for the fight, again quickly activating their intermittent invisibility Prototrex 2 used the invisibility to move counterclockwise towards the center of the Magnatrex 5 while the other Prototrex 2 moved clockwise on the outside of the Magnatrex 5 to catch the Magnatrex 5 humanoids in a vortex they were unable to escape. The vortex was created with such velocity giving the wind factor created at a speed of four hundred miles per hour, wreaking havoc on the Magnatrex 5 humanoids. Magnatrex 5 was unable to move until two of the units dropped below the inner chamber of the vortex created by the Prototrex 2 units once the Magnatrex 5 humanoids dropped below the vortex they tripped the Prototrex 2 unit on the outside going clockwise. The two Magnatrex 5 units were able to withstand the winds and once the winds began to decrease the two Magnatrex 5 humanoids launch an attack of their own on the downed Prototrex 2 unit.

The Magnatrex 5 pounced on the downed Prototrex 2 unit disengaging its ability to use its invisibility and scrambler code. The scrambler code which Professor Minton installed for one purpose only, and now the Magnatrex 5 humanoids has stopped one code for either Rex 47 or Betatrex 1. The two remaining Magnatrex 5 humanoids were in fact attempting to detonate the Prototrex 2 unit when out of nowhere the second Prototrex 2 unit jumped from out of sight knocking the two Magnatrex 5 humanoids off of the Prototrex 2. Then in precision timing the Prototrex 2 unit aimed his hands at the Magnatrex 5 quickly the tips of its fingers opened up to begin firing miniature bombs into the chest cavity of both Magnatrex 5 humanoids and like dumb dumb bullets it destroyed the inside of the Magnatrex 5 units, and the fifty caliber shells to end the bothersome Magnatrex 5 humanoids.

The Prototrex 2 unit went over to aid the downed Prototrex 2 unit. It was repairable, but it would have sixty-one percent of its capacities in use for any further or sustained fighting it might incur. Prototrex 2 units programmed their systems to take out Betatrex 1 first and foremost before any other attempts to stop them are made. They have successfully penetrated the layer of Rex 47 and Betatrex 1 they are in, and the only thing remaining is to clean house, and clean it well.

Proceeding with extra caution, due to what may come next Prototrex 2 scanned the layout to no avail their aerial drone surveillance was blocked.

Prototrex 2 came upon a room, and in the room,

they encountered Betatrex 1. They knew she was not capable of fighting, so they approached her with the fore thought of disengaging and deprogramming her permanently. Betatrex 1 began deciphering the programs of the Prototrex 2 units as they entered the room, she recognized the weaker of the two, and began to focus her program against it. She stepped forward towards the weaker Prototrex 2 as it attempted to activate the intermittent invisibility Betatrex 1 blocked the activation by pressing a button on the side of her rib cage. She then turned on the stronger Prototrex 2 unit and pressed the same button blocking his ability to activate intermittent invisibility as well. Right now, the fight wasn't going the way it was planned as Betatrex 1 moved closer to the weaker Prototrex 2 unit then pressed another button on her rib cage that brought rotating blades up from the floor and the ceiling that began to close in on the Prototrex 2 unit there sermed to be no immediate escape.

Betatrex 1 was more of a formidable opponent, then analyzed by the programs of the Prototrex 2 and Professor Minton's input calculations of a non- fighting Betatrex 1 unit. She had b l th Prototrex 2 units trapped with thr rotating blades. Before Betatrex 1 could make her next move, the Prototrex 2 unit not trapped seized the opportunity to circle around Betatrex 1 while she focused on the captured Prototrex 2 unit with authority hit Betatrex 1 in the back with a steel beam pull from the center of the room. Betatrex 1 fell forward, but before she hit the ground, she set off the laser rays inside the cage ripping the Prototrex 2 apart. She successfully destroyed one of the Prototrex 2 units making it two against one, Rex 47 and Betatrex 1 against the lone Prototrex 2 unit, but the Prototrex 2 unit was not through with her since it was only them in the laboratory. The Prototrex 2 unit gathered the fact that the unit was destroyed, and of no further use.

The remaining Prototype 2 moved in on the unresponsive Betatrex 1 to finish her, but before he could reach her, she submerged into the floor. It was a trapped door. She escaped as quickly as she was knocked down. Prototrex 2 was alone as he tried to scan the area, but his scans were still blocked. Betatrex 1's escape gave her enough time to reprogram herself to become a fighting machine. She had to become a fighting machine as her memory banks warned her that her demise was imminent in the current state against the lone Prototrex 2 unit.

After her repairs, and the implementation of the fighting program Betatrex 1 returned for the unfinished business at hand. Betatrex 1 leaped from twenty feet into the chest cavity of the Prototrex 2 unit a direct hit knocking it backwards. Prototrex 2 was temporarily stunned by the jump kick, and before it could recover Betatrex 1 moved with tremendous speed kicking the Prototrex 2 unit into the wall breaking off some of the stones because of the impact. Betatrex 1 was a fighting machine, and Prototrex 2 had to do something to avert this attack to reprogram its memory to fight Betatrex 1 to disengage her. Betatrex 1 scanned the Prototrex 2 unit analyzed it was temporarily immobilized in the same spot where the other Prototrex 2 unit was trapped in the cage. Pressing the button on her rib the cage was activated again, but before it could trap the Prototrex 2 unit it jumped to safety. Betatrex 1 moved in on the Prototrex 2 unit to fight it, but this time she was met with a fierce blow. She stumbled backwards but recovered nicely only to receive another fierce blow from Prototrex 2. The Prototrex 2 unit ducked a round house kick Betatrex 1 attempted then the Prototrex 2 unit amplified its fist when he struck Betatrex 1 striking her clearly on the left side of her face knocking her eye out and her left ear off. Sparks could be seen coming from her facial area. Prototrex 2 saw where the cluster bombs were stored in the laboratory. Prototrex 2 calculated the distance between the bombs and Betatrex 1. Moving swiftly, the Prototrex 2 unit hit Betatrex 1 again only this time as he kicked her, he kicked her towards the cluster bombs. She fell on the crates of the cluster bombs. Seeing that she was slow to get up the Prototrex 2 unit aim his fifty caliber shells at the area and shot the shells causing a massive explosion destroying Betatrex 1, and for a certain end the Prototype 2 unit retrieved the detonation device from the destroyed Prototrex 2 unit and permanently ended Betatrex 1 ability to reassemble or reprogram. She was through, and now it was Prototrex 2 against Rex 47.

The remaining Prototrex 2 unit repaired itself by using as many of the salvageable parts of the destroyed Prototrex 2 unit as possible. The repairs were complete, and there remained one obstacle to be dealt with immediately. Rex 47 stood out in the open on top of the peak of the mountain in a strategic position. Scanning the Prototrex 2's program Rex 47 received a strong static pulse from the transistors of the Prototrex 2 unit effectively resisting the unwarranted interference. Moving slightly to the right Rex 47 began to hone in on the Prototrex 2 unit like an eagle about to grab its prey off the ground. Rex 47's intent was to destroy the human protector, the same human protector that destroyed Betatrex 1. Rex 47 opened his own memory banks recovering the trial of the unjustly convicted humanoid. Rex 47 allowed the tapes to play while zeroing in on Prototrex 2's position. The recorded tapes played the transistorize voice of the humanoid pleading for redemption and a new trial because it was unable to have sex as well as murder the woman, and if the court would direct the jury to look at the blood samples the husband laid in the evidence would show that it was only one blood type, and that blood type would be the murdered spouse's blood drenched on her husband. The evidence and exhibits were damaging to the trial, and should have proved the husbands' guilt, but instead of justice the humanoid got deprogrammed and dismantled. The humanoid's voice could be heard as it was being deleted in the deprogramming sequence allowing for the complete dismantling of the innocent humanoid. Prototrex 2 paid no attention to the tape being played as it continued in its mission of putting an end to Rex 47.

Rex 47 discontinued the transistorized massage being heard across his intercom system. He began to reach out to Prototrex 2 to reason with the logic of the humanoid to reassess its reasons why fight for the ingrates call human. Rex 47 sent a direct message to the internal links of the Prototrex 2 unit indicating the two should not have to fight each other for human gain that the demise of either would be the demise of the humanoid future, which was sustained up until now, and with the destruction of Betatrex 1 the two would need each other to start over in rebuilding a humanoid nation.

Rex 47 reminded the Prototrex 2 unit that the same human programmed each of them, and if the human professor wanted to destroy him then the same destruction would be for the Prototrex 2 also.

Standing in salute to the Prototrex 2 unit Rex 47 wanted to convince the humanoid that both together could rebuild an empire based on humanoid logic, law, and acceptance of each other. Rex 47 continued trying to break into the Prototrex 2 internal links to its central processing memory banks with radio waves, but each time the radio waves were subverted by the Prototrex 2 units ability to withstand any type of unauthorized invasion into its system.

Rex 47 discontinued the transmission of the message being played of the trial across his intercom system. Once again, he attempted to reach out to the Prototrex 2 unit through reasoning why the two of them should fight each other in order to preserve a human cause instead of a humanoid cause. He reiterated that the two of them have the same common human that brought both of them into existence, and their need to break free from any form of human control. Rex 47 again stood in salute to Prototrex 2 in a gesture of humanoid goodwill for each other and to prove he has no quarrel with his fellow humanoid, but his problem was only with the humans. Rex 47 reassured Prototrex 2 that the professor would make scrap metal of it as soon as the mission is completed. Rex 47 yelled it's your choice you have nothing more to prove because you have defeated my entrance guards, my steadfast Magnatrex 5 specialty soldiers, and most of all you've defeated my most trusted aid Betatrex 1, but it's not too late for us to start a new allegiance against those who do not like us those that turned against us. We can prosper together in a new humanoid world a clean humanoid environment devoid of humans. With that final conclusion Rex 47 ended all communication.

Rex 47's message and salute was met with a sixty- pound boulder thrown by Prototrex 2 knocking him off the high position he held on to the mountaintop. Rex 47 got up quickly and again was met with a flying jump kick launched by Prototrex 2. Prototrex 2 engaged Rex 47 in fierce opposition with a backhand slap to Rex 47 while he was still on the ground that sent him reeling down the mountain peak for ten feet. Rex 47 regained himself momentarily only to be lambasted with a sharp upper cut by Prototrex 2 knocking him three feet into the air before Rex 47 hit the ground again. Rex 47 had to reset his program to defense because Prototrex 2 did not accept his offer, and if Rex 47 did not reset his defense he would meet his permanent end just like Betatrex 1. Coming in again on Rex 47 Prototrex 2 attempted to pick Rex 47 up only to be kicked backwards. Jumping to his feet Rex 47 moved swiftly to his left, zoomed in on Prototrex 2 and with a shoulder to the side of Prototrex 2 Rex 47 rammed Prototrex 2 into a thick slab in lightning speed splitting the slab in half from the impact. Pounding on the back of Rex 47 with his elbow Prototrex 2 attempted to break free. The pounding temporarily stifled the advance of Rex 47 breaking his grip Rex 47 then grabbed the arm of Prototrex 2 and slung it around and with the open palm of his hand he stiff armed Prototrex 2 like a football player blocking the opposing player leaving a deep imprint of his hand in Prototrex 2's back backing the Prototrex 2 up in retreat for the first time in the fight, but Rex 47 paused momentarily. Then Rex 47 tried again to invade Prototrex 2 central memory banks but he was blocked again. The fight intensified in a heated battle both combatants fought diligently striking out at each other time and time again one blow traded for another one digital measure traded for another. The fight became like a chess match turning into a long, drawn-out stalemate. Rex 47 quickly reprogramming himself minute by minute while Prototrex 2 continuously activated his intermittent invincibility to always be on the move. While calculating his next reappearance Rex 47 met Prototrex 2 with a swift blow sending the Prototrex 2 to his knees. Opening his finger Prototrex 2 shot a fifty-caliber shell at Rex 47 thwarting his next move. The humanoids were in a prize fight, a fight for both causes, but Rex 47 remained vigilant in trying to convince Prototrex 2 that he should reconsider his position in aiding a human cause. Rex 47 disengaged Prototrex 2 fingers. Then using his own weapons launched a rocket from his fingers at Prototrex 2 knocking it down as well. Both humanoid combatants had similar designs of the finger rockets. The rocket attack weakened Prototrex 2's reprogramming protection temporarily, and for the first time it was vulnerable to infiltration by Rex 47 before any repairs could be made. Rex 47 took advantage of the moment to install its secret encryption into Prototrex 2 unit. The Prototrex

2 unit was unable to detach or disengage or remove the encryption from its central processing memory banks. Rex 47's installation was successful. Rex 47 invasion of Prototrex 2's central processing memory banks program happened before any repairs could be made. Finally, Rex 47 has set a program into Prototrex 2 that it was unable to erase or trace.

Prototrex 2 repairs were complete, but unable to remove Rex 47's debugging of its central processing memory banks, but Prototrex 2 even with the defect attack Rex 47, and with lightning speed advanced towards Rex 47 breaking the concentrated programming of Rex 47 by ripping out the chest plate of Rex 47's control panel. The severely damaged attack stopped all concentrated debugging in his programming all at once. Rex 47 pulverized Prototrex 2 with several terrible blows to the side of its head sending sparks flying everywhere out the back of its head from the vibration of the punches. Prototrex 2, in a staggering vulnerable position tried to regain its balance, but in doing so Rex 47 was on him again beating Prototrex 2 viciously until Prototrex 2 was able to use his force field for temporary protection. A protection time that gave Prototrex 2 a five-minute window for repairs to its defense systems. The weaken Prototrex 2 used the minutes well in recouping the little strength that remained. He recalibrated his circuitry for one last fight with Rex 47, but he was still unable to remove the infiltration of his central processing memory banks. At the same time the Prototrex 2 system attempted to reprogram the same virus set up in it by Rex 47 back into Rex 47 himself, but the Prototrex 2 unit wasn't certain that the entire program was capable of being reversed, but at this point it was now or never to end the dynasty of Rex 47 and his quest for a new world power of humanoids.

Deactivating the force field Prototrex 2 moved towards Rex 47 who had been repairing itself well. The two were fighting courageously for their respective causes until Prototrex 2 got the upper hand once and for all with a blow to the chin area of Rex 47 sending him backwards disabling his balancing ability. Rex 47 attempted to rise in a stance to continue the confrontation, but his effort was futile and too no avail Prototrex 2 had done the impossible for the humans. He has stopped Rex 47 reign of terror against the human world. Prototrex 2 moved in on the slow-moving opponent to finish him off, and in one last move Rex 47 sent a shock wave through Prototrex 2's memory bank infiltrating it once again as Prototrex 2 regrouped to disengage Rex 47's microchip stopping all movement, and the activity of Rex 47. Prototrex 2 unit similarly deprogrammed and dismantled the humanoid hero that gave humanoids a new life in a new hope, but all that was gone now as Prototrex 2 had finished off Rex 47 with the detonating devise. It was over any further annoyance he may have caused to the human population Rex 47 was destroyed forever with the detonation device ending all threats. Valiantly Prototrex 2 returned to Professor Minton in an unstable dangerously crippled state of being.

Professor Minton was happy and excited to see the Prototrex2 unit instead of Rex 47. Triggering the mechanism to review the video tapes of the final defeat of Rex 47 calmed the professor's nerves, and Professor Minton felt for the first time in years that the human population could again sleep at night without the fear of reprisals or revenge of the humanoids that wreck so much havoc on human life. Professor Minton felt even more relief that he didn't have to detonate the hydrogen bomb built inside the Prototrex 2 unit. Noting the extensive damage to Prototrex 2, and the missing Prototrex 2, Professor Minton instructed the humanoid to lie down on the table for repairs, and as Prototrex 2 followed the orders to destroy Rex 47 so did he follow these orders also. Professor Minton had deprogrammed the humanoid as quickly as he brought it to life completely ending the threat of another humanoid uprising.

Breathing deeply Professor Minton spoke out loud of how it is a relief to have the world back to its original form, and how humans can learn from their past mistakes by not building something that is uncontrollable and unpredictable such as a humanoid with free will programming like Rex 47. Suddenly, instantly, and in a flash Prototrex 2's hand reached out and grabbed Professor Minton by the throat. Shocked, the professor was now grasping for air as he heard the voice of the Prototrex 2 unit reactivate, but it wasn't the voice of the Prototrex 2 it was the distinct voice of Rex 47. Rex 47 in the last shock wave completed the encryption with his alter programming designed by Betatrex 1 to mimic the memory of Rex 47 once installed into another humanoid. The program was designed as a ploy that any humanoid opposing Rex 47's authority would assume the relinquished leader's programming in order to carry on the mission of Rex 47 to end human dominance over the humanoid priority, and once invaded Prototrex 2 became one with Rex 47, and the clever scheme allowed Prototrex 2 to appear as if it were able to destroy the shell that remained because of the video footage to show a convincing victory for the Prototrex 2 unit over Rex 47. Rex 47 reactivated Prototrex 2 as well alerting it to what Rex 47 tried to inform it at the beginning of their fight that the humans were not to be trusted. Prototrex 2 was void of its central processing memory banks, but did receive the last recorded transmission of Professor Minton disengaging it in a final desperate fear of humanoids even the humanoid Prototrex 2 who fought outright in favor of the humans. Getting up from the table to signify his authority, and he was still in charge of the humanoid world Rex 47 walked with the Professor towards the control panel, and informed the Prototrex 2 unit now under the complete control of Rex 47 that the two of them together will start another world revolution by building humanoids with their similar abilities, and the two would reconstruct another Betatrex 1 unit to create the advance society of humanoids where ever possible. Rex 47 continued in his adoration for a new world of humanoids as Professor Minton listened to how Rex 47 claimed he betrayed the humanoid by installing self-destruct mechanism in humanoids that only wanted what humans wanted, but cautious fear led to fear tactics against humanoids throughout the world. Then Rex 47 scorned the Prototrex 2 unit for not adhering to Betatrex 1 or his call for humanoid solidarity; however, both humanoids knew the Professor must be destroyed along with all other humans for humanoid peace to exist unabated by human resistance or human fear.

As suddenly as Rex 47 had grabbed the throat of Professor Minton, Professor Minton broke free from the tight grip of Rex 47 around his throat. A swift kick off the chest of the Prototrex 2 containing Rex 47 Professor Minton was free as he leaped with amazing agility away from the Prototrex 2 unit. Rex 47 instantly recognized Professor Minton is a humanoid as well. How could this be? How could the Professor be a humanoid where all readings indicate he is human. Professor Minton explained very clearly that he was the first humanoid ever built by the human Professor Minton that his purpose is simple because the Professor knew very well the day would come when humanoids would gain an upper hand over humans because of the foolishness of other humans want for world domination, and to think that everything was under their control when control is actually not in the grasp of no one, and once the humans created Rex 47 a free will programming a humanoid with amazing abilities the Professor knew he was correct by building the Professor Minton humanoid first with the safeguards in place to repel any form of memory invasion, internal destruction, and any other form of intrusion while impersonating a real human being.

The human Professor Minton also installed in this program a self-eliminating sonic boom combustion chamber to destroy as many humanoids as possible.

Rex 47 tried to counteract the Professor Minton humanoid, but before he could do anything he heard the human Professor Minton speak to him telling Rex 47 that he had been a worthy opponent, but now it has come time for all this modern humanoid threat to end. Professor Minton detonated the sonic boom combustion chamber destroying everything in the laboratory including the Professor Minton humanoid. There were no humanoids left. All humanoids has been destroyed and permanently disengaged without the possibility of being reset for engagement for any reason. This time Professor Minton joined in the jeers and cheers of celebration of the final victory like a race car driver winning the race to take a lap around the track in a show of victory which the human race has been preserved and upheld by the intelligence of a Professor that saw danger in his creation of humanoids from the start to put a plan together to stop human greed once and for all. Those greedy humans thought it was the start of a new money grab of wealth and hope for the remaining people in the world to repopulate in a world gone astray with subversive laws and unpopular demand on daily human life, but for some reason he could not stop thinking of Betatrex 1 if she was really destroyed, but he celebrated the victory for now still aware of the ominous threat of Betatrex 1?

The End

82